Steven the Bear Learns How to Camp

Written by Scott Hall
Illustrated by Madison Brake
Special Guest Contributor Jim Demarest

NEW YORK
LONDON · NASHVILLE · MELBOURNE · VANCOUVER

Steven the Bear Learns How to Camp

© 2023 Written by Scott Hall   Illustrated by Madison Brake

All rights reserved. No portion of this book may be reproduced, stored in a retrieval system, or transmitted in any form or by any means—electronic, mechanical, photocopy, recording, scanning, or other—except for brief quotations in critical reviews or articles, without the prior written permission of the publisher.

Published in New York, New York, by Morgan James Publishing. Morgan James is a trademark of Morgan James, LLC. www.MorganJamesPublishing.com

Proudly distributed by Ingram Publisher Services.

*Thank you to Peter Hall for the expertise and
Jim Demarest for the heart.*

ISBN 9781636980027 paperback
ISBN 9781636980034 ebook
ISBN 9781636980041 hardcover
Library of Congress Control Number: 2022941511

Cover Design by:
Madison Brake

Interior Design by:
Chris Treccani
www.3dogcreative.net

Morgan James is a proud partner of Habitat for Humanity Peninsula and Greater Williamsburg. Partners in building since 2006.

Get involved today! Visit MorganJamesPublishing.com/giving-back

"I'm so excited that we're going to learn how to camp with Uncle Gray Jay," says Steven. "He knows all about camping and being outside."

"He also knows how to make our trip fun and safe," says Lily.

"Good morning Bear Bunch, I'm Uncle Gray Jay. I'm excited to take you all on this amazing adventure into the outdoors. I want to introduce you to my rules of camping and enjoying nature without harming it. We have 7 simple rules, and I will make them easy to remember by using hand signals."

Rule 1—Write down your plan so people know where you're going.

Rule 2—Make sure you stay on the path.

Rule 3—Make sure you scoop up all your trash. Pack it in, pack it out.

Hayden the Bobcat asks, "Do all bears scoop in the woods?"

"They sure do," says Uncle Gray Jay. "That's how we keep the forest clean and safe for all the animals."

Rule 4—We are going to take pictures, draw or paint the fun things we see.

Rule 5—When you're on the trail, say hi and be friendly.

Rule 6—Be on the lookout for animals.

Rule 7—Make sure you put your tent on a flat surface.

"Those are my camping rules, Bear Bunch. We are now ready to start our adventure!"

Steven the Bear takes out his note pad and writes down their plan.

1. Start at Carter Trail at 9:00 in the morning.
2. Hike 3 miles to Lake Sydney.
3. If we don't make a lot of stops, we should be at the lake at 10:00 in the morning.
4. Have fun by the lake.
5. Spend 1 night under the stars.
6. Leave Lake Sydney at 11:00 in the morning.
7. Meet Grandma Gigi and Grandpa Bear at Carter Trail at 12:00, just in time for lunch.
8. Give a copy of our plan to Grandpa Bear.

Everyone loves the plan.

"I can't wait to sleep under the stars and make s'mores," says Archy the Wolf.

The Bear Bunch is off on their adventure! Their first stop is at Kady's Camping Supplies and Orchids to pick up some snacks: Cheetos for Archy, Swedish Fish for Jack, chocolate caramel for Lily, spicy Takis for Hayden, and American cheese for Stella.

"Hey, Uncle Gray Jay, look! She's using rule 4. She's painting a picture of that flower instead of picking it."

"You're right! That's my friend Kady. She loves nature and knows all the rules," says Uncle Gray Jay.

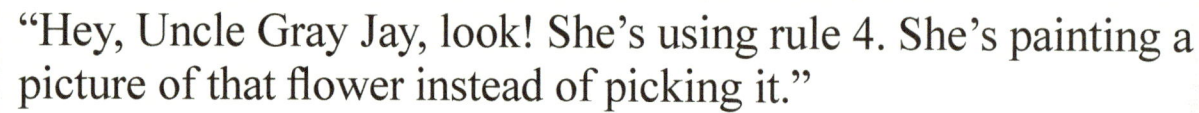

"Hi everyone!" says Kady. "You know rule 4 is one of my favorites. I love to see nature and all its beauty. If you pick a flower, it is only pretty for a short time. That's why I like to paint pictures of the things that are special to me."

Stella asks, "Kady, can I paint a picture of your beautiful orchids?"

"Of course you can, sweetie," says Kady, whispering in her ear. "This is my favorite type of flower!"

How many orchids does Kady have on the table?

After getting a few snacks for the trail, the Bear Bunch is on their way to Lake Sydney.

Hayden says, "Hey everyone, remember the second rule? Stay on the trail. Grandpa Bear says, 'If you stay on the trail you won't fail.'"

"I know it's not our trash but maybe someone accidentally dropped it or didn't remember rule 3—scoop your trash," says Archy. "Grandma Gigi says trash in the wild does not make her smile."

As they are heading up the trail, they see Johnnie the Elk coming down the trail and they all wave hello.

Lily says, "That's rule number 5—wave and be friendly."

"I like your whistle," says Stella.

"Thank you very much," says Johnnie. "I always have it with me when I'm camping."

Johnnie's antlers remind Hayden of rule 6—be on the lookout for animals. Can you find the squirrel? How about the porcupine?

The Bear Bunch finally makes it to Lake Sydney. It is beautiful.

Uncle Gray Jay says, "Now it's time to set up our tents. Does anyone remember rule 7?"

"I sure do," says Jack. "Make sure your tent is on a flat surface."

Lily reminds everyone, "Remember what Grandpa Bear says: 'When you're looking for a place to put your tent, ants and rocks are like a pair of smelly socks.'"

Everyone has a great day and now it is time to relax and have fun.

Hayden practices his handstands.

Lily plays her ukulele.

Jack writes in his journal about all the fun they are having.

Archy feeds the ducks with the corn he has in his backpack. How many ducks does he feed?

Stella makes a new friend and enjoys some cloud watching.

What do these clouds look like to you? Can you find all three?

After dinner, they all circle around the fire. What do you think they had for dessert? You're right! S'mores!

The stars look like shining diamonds in the sky.

"I guess it's time to turn in, Bear Bunch," says Uncle Gray Jay. "I will take care of the fire; you guys tuck into your tents."

With the Bear Bunch all tucked in, they drift to sleep thinking about the fun they had today and the fun they will have on the hike home in the morning.

Pleasant dreams, Bear Bunch.

The End!

S'MORE FACTS

BEARS

Bears hibernate, or sleep, during the winter. Their nap time can sometimes last 100 days! Be glad you're not a bear and enjoy your naps.

Their footprints look like this:

FOXES

Foxes have amazing hearing. They can hear a clock ticking from over 120 feet! That's about the same distance as 20 bathtubs lined up end to end.

Their footprints look like this:

RABBITS

Rabbits sweat from only their feet! They must have really sweaty socks (pee-eww)!

Bunnies make these kinds of footprints:

WOLVES

Wolves will eat apples, pears, and berries; even they know they need to eat their fruits and vegetables.

These are what their footprints look like:

RACCOONS

Raccoons love to eat just about anything. It makes them great for swapping lunches.

These are what their footprints, or tracks, look like:

BOBCATS

Bobcats use their whiskers to help them judge whether a hole is big enough to fit through. This makes them great at hide and seek!

Their footprints, or tracks, look like this:

BLUEBIRDS

Bluebirds are symbols of happiness. They even wrote a song about it: "Mr. Bluebird On My Shoulder."

These are their footprints, or tracks:

GRAY JAYS

Gray Jays will carry food with their feet, unlike some other birds that carry food in their beaks. They know not to talk with their mouth full.

These are what their footprints, or tracks, look like:

ELK

Elk can weigh up to 700 pounds, but they can still jump up to 8 feet in the air. You would want one on your basketball team.

These are what their footprints, or tracks, look like:

CATS

Cats can't taste sweetness, so no need to share your S'mores with a cat.

Their footprints, or tracks, look like this:

LONG LIVE THE ORCHID!
Orchids are the largest family of flowering plants. With more than 25,000 species, there are more orchids on the planet than mammals and birds. They can also live up to 100 years!

STEVEN THE BEAR'S NUMBER 1 S'MORES TIP

Steven the Bear says, "I like to use Keebler Fudge Stripes cookies for my S'mores. I simply roast my delicious marshmallow and put it between the cookies. They have it all, cookie, chocolate, and smiles. Sometimes crackers crack funny and the chocolate bars are too big and hard to unwrap. They are super easy to pack when you are off to enjoy the outdoors or just enjoying s'mores in your backyard."

Find Steven and the Bear Bunch online!
(With your parent's permission)
Go to the website to print FREE coloring pages.
www.StevenTheBear.com

We would love to hear from you!
Email us at:
steven@steventhebear.com

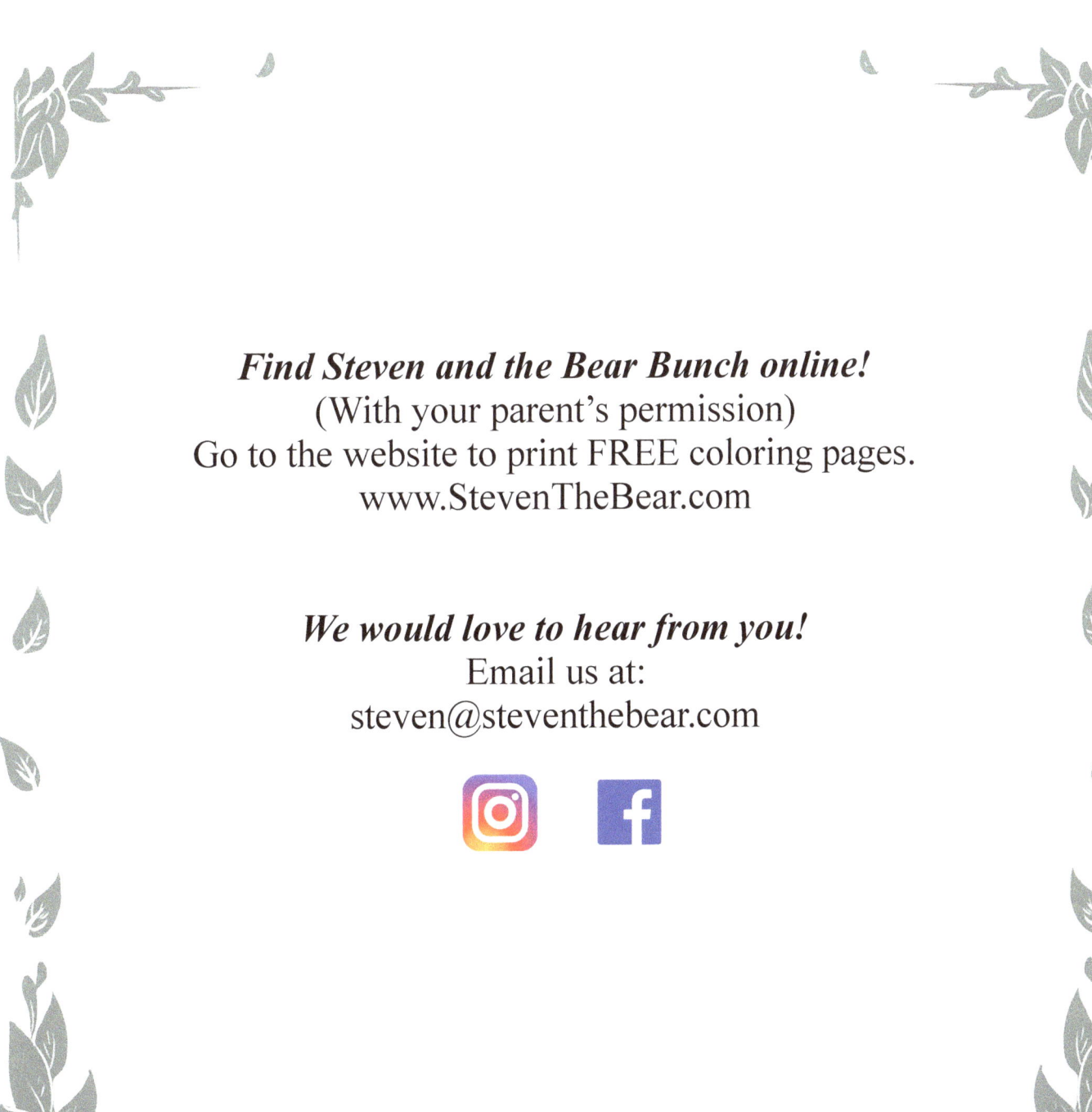

About the Author

Steven the Bear Learns How to Camp is the second book in a series for Scott Hall. He is not your typical author kind of guy. He served in the Air Force for 28 years flying the A-10, F-15, and the F-16. Steven's adventures are inspired by true events from camping trips, hikes, and his grandchildren. Scott is known for lots of corny Dad/Bear jokes (the grandkids call him Bear). Look for this first book, *How Steven the Bear Invented S'mores*, and, coming soon, *Steven the Bear's First Airplane Ride*.

About the Illustrator

Madison Brake is an illustrator, scribbler, and cat enthusiast currently surviving in the swamplands of Florida. She draws inspiration from animals, fairy tales, and the natural world.

S'more Background on the Book

I have had the pleasure of working with Jim "Boots" Demarest for many years. He is a patriot, father, business owner, and author. I am honored to remember his wife Karysia in this book as our new character Kady.
—*Scott Hall*

A free ebook edition is available with the purchase of this book.

To claim your free ebook edition:

1. Visit MorganJamesBOGO.com
2. Sign your name CLEARLY in the space
3. Complete the form and submit a photo of the entire copyright page
4. You or your friend can download the ebook to your preferred device

Print & Digital Together Forever.

Snap a photo   Free ebook   Read anywhere